C.V. Aramakutu

LOOPY LUCY

FLYING
WITH
HUBBLE

**For my daughter Amelia.
Explore with courage.**

Loopy Lucy by C.V. Aramakutu

Published by C.V. Aramakutu
Palmerston North
New Zealand

Cover Illustration © 2018 Sophie Blokker

ISBN-13: 978-1717403667

1
JOURNEY TO JUNK

"Stop laughing at me you leotard-loving losers," Lucy yelled at her gym class, who were mocking her attempts on the balance beam. "I don't get this gym thing, anyway. What purpose does walking in a straight line have?" she said to her teacher, Miss Knuckles. "And the beam isn't even straight!"

It was the third time this week she'd been forced into doing roly-polys, like a five-year-old, and jumping over a stupid wooden horse – which, by the way, didn't even look like a horse. And each time, she'd been humiliated by her wobbly knees and lack of gymnastic talent.

3

Today was by far the worst day of the three. Miss Knuckles had insisted that Lucy complete a walk on the balance beam in front of the entire class. It wasn't her fault she'd failed a dozen times; she was being taunted by the old ten-centimetre wooden beam disguised as a tightrope! *How on earth can I balance on that?*

As she sat on the floor after her most recent spectacular fail, Miss Knuckles could see she was a lost cause.

"Okay, Lucy, that's enough then. You really do need to try harder."

"TRY HARDER?" Lucy bellowed, her voice echoing off the gymnasium walls. "HOW COULD I HAVE TRIED HARDER? I FELL OFF THE DAMN THING TWELVE TIMES!"

Oh no, Lucy thought to herself. *I'm in trouble.*

Lucy had never before yelled at her teacher, she had always been a good student. But today was different – very different. Because last night,

Lucy had experienced something so terrifyingly strange that she hadn't dared go back to sleep.

It was eight o'clock in the evening, and Lucy's mum, a brilliant astronomer and professor at Reddington University, flopped onto Lucy's overly bright – some would say fluorescent – pink duvet cover.

Lucy's mum was beautiful, with long wavy brown hair and sharp blue eyes. Lucy was proud to look a lot like her – except for her eyes, which Mum called milk chocolate eyes.

"What a day I've had, my darling," sighed Mum. She worked long hours, and Lucy always missed her. Most nights she would be asleep when Mum came home from work.

"Today I spoke to my class about space junk," she said. "Do you know what space junk is?"

Lucy was intrigued but a bit confused – Mum didn't usually talk about her work. "Space junk?"

"Yeah, it's really quite interesting. There are thousands, even millions of manmade pieces of rubbish just orbiting around Earth! I'm not talking about old apple cores or dirty nappies, of course – I mean spacey things, like unused satellites and old spacecraft engines; even tools that astronauts have let go of on spacewalks!"

Lucy was amazed, and kind of disgusted. She'd had no idea space had its own rubbish tip!

"So, my darling, you'd better be careful on the walk to school tomorrow, just in case a space hammer donks you on the head," Mum said with a smirk.

Lucy raised her eyebrows in alarm. "Are you serious?"

"Ha ha, no. There's no need to worry. Any junk that falls from the sky usually lands in the ocean, or somewhere remote. Although there was this one time … No, I'm teasing. That's enough for tonight, Lucy."

"MUM! Can you tell me more about space tomorrow night?"

"We'll see, my darling. Goodnight." She turned out the light above Lucy's bed and closed the door behind her.

Lucy snuggled into her disco duvet with a wide smile on her face. *I hope she gets home early tomorrow night too.*

BANG BANG BANG!

In the middle of the night, Lucy woke suddenly to a commotion downstairs.

The wind is banging the back door in the laundry. No worries, Dad will close it.

After a few moments of silence – *Dad must have sorted it* – Lucy pulled the duvet over her head and drifted back to sleep.

BANG BANG BANG!

What the?

Lucy jumped up, furious at having to drag herself out of bed to shut the back door. "Bunch of lazies," she mumbled to herself as she shuffled down the stairs, along the hall, and through into the laundry.

It was dark in the laundry … really dark. Lucy guessed it must have been about two a.m. She reached out, moving her hand around the dark space in front of her, searching for the door handle.

"Argh!" she squeaked, stubbing her fingers on the metal handle. *It's closed? That's strange.*

She stopped for a second, squeezing the pain from her throbbing fingers. Perhaps she'd dreamt the noise.

She turned away and headed back to bed.

BANG BANG BANG!

Lucy almost jumped out of her skin with fright. She'd only watched two scary movies in all her eleven years, but she knew one thing for sure

– DON'T OPEN THE DOOR!

Don't be a scaredy cat, Lucy. It might just be the stray cat that was sleeping in the hedge by the letterbox last week.

"Kitty, Kitty," she whispered through the door.

There was no answering meow from the other side.

Hmmm. Maybe I'll just have a little peek.

Lucy gently pulled on the handle, opening a small gap, making sure to stand behind it just in case the cat got a fright too and jumped up at her.

Nothing. No cat.

Lucy opened the door wide to get a better look.

Nothing.

As she quietly inched the door shut again, a gust of wind swirled through and snatched one of the socks hanging on the clothes horse, whipping it outside, where it landed on the second step down to the garden path. Without thinking, Lucy leaped out to grab the sock … and you won't believe what happened next!

2

HAMMER HEADACHE

The backyard had vanished! Lucy looked down to see her feet floating above nothing. She froze, expecting her body to fall into the dark, empty space beneath her.

Looking up again, she couldn't believe the sight that met her eyes. In front of her, twinkling in the blackness of the void, were millions of tiny sparkling lights that looked just like stars.

Lucy panicked and stepped back into the laundry, stumbling and falling on her bottom.

The bright lights had disappeared, and the back door was now all she could see. Dazed, she shook her head and tugged at her tangled bed hair, desperate to wake up from this nightmare.

But her curiosity got the better of her, and without thinking too much about it Lucy stood up, whipped the door open again, and stepped back into the glittering darkness. She looked around, mesmerized by its beauty.

Then she saw something emerge from the vast space ahead, travelling in her direction.

What is that?

She squinted, adjusting her eyes as the object came closer, growing bigger.

Hang on, that looks like a hammer …

DONK!

BEEP BEEP BEEP!

Lucy jolted awake and slammed her hand down onto her alarm clock.

Phew, it was just a stupid dream. To be sure, she shuffled downstairs, along the hall and into the laundry then peeked out the back door. It was a gorgeous day and she was comforted by the bright sunlight shining through the leaves of the lemon trees that lined the back fence.

Lucy's tummy grumbled at the thought of fresh, sweet, homemade lemonade. She dragged her tired body back down the hall and into the kitchen, where Mum was sitting drinking her morning coffee.

"Did you hear that banging last night, Mum?"

"Oh, good morning, Lucy."

"Mum, did you hear it?" Lucy hated it when Mum ignored her questions.

"No, Lucy. Get out of the wrong side of the bed, did we?"

"Whatever, I'm just tired," Lucy mumbled.

Mum put her mug in the sink and used a cloth to wipe up the coffee ring she always managed to leave on the counter. She kissed the top of Lucy's bird's-nest hair. "I've got to go now, sweetie. Your dad's already at work, so don't forget to lock the front door on your way out."

"Okay, Mum."

"Your brother will walk you to school. Please remind him to take his lunch. Yesterday he had to eat baked beans from the school staffroom and I didn't hear the end of it all night!"

Zac was four years older than Lucy – fifteen going on five, she often teased. He was shorter than the average teen, but super strong, and he often boasted about being the next Mr Olympia. He spent more time in the garage pretending to lift heavy weights and looking in the mirror, than he did doing his school work. Despite their obvious differences, Lucy secretly adored him.

"Here's your lunch, Zacadoodle," she said, handing him a can of baked beans, trying desperately not to giggle.

"Ha-ha, you're so funny," Zac replied sarcastically. "Let's go Lucky Ducky." He bolted out the door, leaving the beans on the bench.

Lucy slipped them into her bag, hoping for another opportunity to tease him at school.

Old North High School wasn't far; just a few blocks'

walk, past the fish and chip shop which fried up the best hot dogs on a stick – Lucy's favourite – then around the corner where the snarly dog barked at Lucy every morning through a hole in the fence. Then only fifty metres more, which gave just enough time for her heart rate to drop back down to normal … and to remember that she had gymnastics first up. *Oh no!*

"Hey, Luce!" a red-headed girl yelled out from across the courts. She zipped over to Lucy like a bullet.

"Hi, Bonny."

15

Lucy and Bonny had been best friends since their very first day at primary school, when they'd bonded over play dough, and raspberry jam sandwiches.

"You all right, Luce? What's up with your hair?"

Lucy put her hand to her head, and realised that in her fluster that morning, she'd forgotten to brush it!

Great, I can be exhausted and look like an unloved Barbie doll all day too!

"I'm okay, couldn't find my hairbrush." She decided not to tell Bonnie about last night. Who would believe such an outrageous tale anyway? "I've got to get changed for gym class, I'll see you at morning tea, Bon."

Lucy shuffled off to the gym changing rooms, where she wet her hands under the tap and ran her fingers through her tangled mess of hair. Luckily, she found an old hair tie in the bottom of her bag and pulled her hair back into a messy bun – more mess than bun, for sure!

Old North High was okay, Lucy thought, although it could be a little scary sometimes – not many high schools started at Year 7, but there wasn't much choice in Abeltown. It was that or home-school, which was not something Lucy or her parents were keen on.

There was a mix of cool kids and not-so-cool kids, plus the weird kids and the nerdy kids. Lucy wasn't really in any of these groups; instead she had friends in all of them. And Bonnie was her bestie, of course.

On days when humiliation in gym class threatened, it was great to know that not everyone would be laughing at her!

3

MRS PRIERS

"It's not my fault, Miss Knuckles!"

Oh no, I've yelled at my teacher again. Shut your mouth, Lucy.

Miss Knuckles froze. From the way her jaw dropped, you'd think she'd just spotted a long-extinct animal. She was used to such disrespect from some of the children in her class, but Lucy wasn't one of them. For the first time ever, Lucy was given her marching orders. "Off you go to the principal's office. Maybe you can explain to her why you gave up on the beam." Miss Knuckles' voice was stern and a little shaky.

Lucy's heart stopped beating for a

moment, and her neck sunk into her shoulders like a turtle retreating into its shell. Without another word she made her way out of the hall, staring at the floor, past her sneering classmates.

As she walked along the corridor she muttered under her breath. "Gave up … whatever! I can't even see the beam properly. Not that she cares."

The school office area wasn't as scary as Lucy had expected. There was no dark cavern awaiting her – it was quite lovely, really. The walls were covered in students' bright painted artworks; proud teachers showing off their teaching skills! Miss Beach, the office lady, was there too. She always wore her hair in a neat ballerina bun, keeping her fringe from falling into her eyes with two red clips.

"Hi, Lucy, what can I do for you?" she asked politely.

"My teacher sent me here to see Mrs

Priers."

Lucy was rarely in the office, but when she was, it was usually for something good, like getting a big gold star sticker on her work.

"Mrs Priers? Oh, okay Lucy. Take a seat over there and I'll let her know you're here." Miss Beach looked just as surprised as Miss Knuckles had in the gym! Lucy smiled nervously and took a seat on the leather two-seater, which was framed by the art displays. The seat was awfully sticky under her sweaty legs. *I hope I don't get stuck to it!*

Lucy had little time to think about what to say, as Mrs Priers came out almost immediately and invited her into her office.

PHRRRT!

The sound of Lucy peeling herself off the seat was too fart-like to ignore. Miss Beach let out a sly giggle and Lucy's face turned the colour of pickled beetroot!

"I was stuck to the seat," she said swiftly in

embarrassment.

Principal Priers wore a fake smile along with her mauve pant suit – which Lucy assumed she must have found in a thrift shop. She wasn't too scary. Firm but fair, she said of herself – often. Her short blonde hair curled in a way that made it look like someone had poured a bowl of spaghetti over her head. One day, she'd made the mistake of wearing a brown and red woollen beret, so her head had looked like a bowl of spaghetti bolognaise. The school jokesters had had fun with that one for days!

"So, Lucy, why have you been sent here?" Mrs Priers asked.

"Well, I kept falling off the beam in gym class, and I got angry I guess. I was trying, though!"

"Hmm, I don't think Miss Knuckles would send you here for simply falling off the beam. Is there anything else you'd like to share?"

"I may have raised my voice a little," Lucy confessed.

"Yelled?" Mrs Priers was a pro at quickly squeezing information out of people.

"I yelled at Miss Knuckles because she said I wasn't trying, but I really was."

Mrs Priers dug deeper. "Okay, is that the only reason why you yelled?"

Lucy was reluctant to tell the whole truth, so she decided that half would do. "I couldn't see the beam very well, it was blurry."

"I see. Maybe I need to ring your parents to discuss this problem …"

My parents? MY PARENTS! How did my tongue get me into this much trouble?

Lucy started to panic. "I'm really sorry, I'll go right now and apologise to–"

Mrs Priers interrupted her. "I need to talk to your parents about the problem with your eyes."

Lucy started to feel a little relieved. "Oh, yeah, okay," she responded quietly, hoping she was no longer in trouble.

"But you can indeed write an apology letter to Miss Knuckles before you return to class. Yelling at teachers is not acceptable, Lucy."

There it was, the punishment. Quite mild, really. Lucy had more worrying thoughts … *am I going blind? At least that would explain the strange happenings last night!*

4

GOOGLY EYES

It was a "slow walk home" kind of a day. Lucy wondered if Mrs Priers had talked to her parents only about her vision problem, or if she'd told them the whole horrific gym class story. Her day really couldn't have got much worse, on top of last night's weirdness, which was even more worrying.

Her jumbled thoughts were interrupted by the smell of frying hot dogs leaking out from the open fish and chip shop door. *Surely after the last twenty-four hours I deserve a hot dog?*

While Lucy waited for her food, Zac peeked his head around the shop door and whispered, "Dad texted me, he's waiting for you at home." Then he added, "Ha ha, you're in trouble, aren't yah, Lucky Ducky!" A big brother never misses a chance to tease!

"Yeah, whatever, Zac." Lucy didn't have the energy to care.

"See you at home, sis," he said, now looking like he felt a little sorry for her.

It was after four o'clock by the time Lucy walked in the front door. Her dad, a fire-fighter, had been home since finishing his shift. He was a tall, broad-shouldered man, with bushy black hair that always looked like a trodden-down shaggy rug by the end of his working day.

He must have been to a fire. Lucy pictured him in his fireman's helmet. Dad was a gentle giant with a soft heart – a fact that Lucy hoped to take advantage of today.

"I got a call from your principal. Come and sit down."

A greeting and a command all in one. This should be good. She shuddered.

Lucy and Dad had a good relationship. They talked a lot on the phone when he was stuck at the fire station, awaiting the next sausage sizzle gone wrong. His shift work meant they didn't spend much time together, but the phone calls helped. Sometimes Lucy rang just to see what the fire station was having for tea – savoury mince and mashed spuds, usually!

"I called your mother at work to tell her about your little incident at school today," he began.

"Yip," tweeted Lucy.

"I need a little more than 'yip', my girl." His tone was angry.

"I didn't mean to yell or be rude, Dad. I'm sorry."

"Good. It won't be happening again – do you hear me?" His huge shoulders were in full parent mode.

"Okay." Lucy slumped deep into the couch pillows.

Zac piped up from across the room. "Mum said you have an eye appointment in half an hour, Lucky. She's coming to get you now."

Zac the messenger was at it again. Lucy couldn't wait until she had her own phone, so he could keep his big nose out of her business!

Dad patted her on the head. "You'll be all right, kid."

"Yeah, you'll be sweet as, googly eyes!" Zac dodged the pillow that flew at him from across the room.

HONK HONK! The blue family four-wheel drive pulled into the driveway. Lucy ran out and jumped into the front passenger seat.

"Hi, Mum," she said softly.

"Hi, sweetie. Let's get this sorted quickly, eh? I have a lecture at six o'clock." Mum was

27

always in a rush; so much to do and never any time to do it. *Of course, she gets an appointment straight away, she's so powerful like that.* Lucy marvelled at Mum's ability to juggle everything. *So, no time to bring up the yelling incident – I hope.*

Forty-five minutes later, Lucy was home clutching a brand-new pair of hideous temporary glasses, ready for the barrage of "four eyes" jokes from Zac.

"Before you say anything, protein head, I'm not wearing them, so shut up!" Lucy burst into tears and ran up to her room, then lay on her bed for hours. Her favourite book, *Matilda*, by Roald Dahl, remained unopened in a silent act of protest.

Lucy jumped at the sound of her bedroom door opening. She was still on edge after today's chaos.

"It's me, sweetie. Are you okay?" Mum slid gently into bed next to her. "Dad told me you were upset about your glasses."

"I don't want to talk about it," Lucy snapped.

She knew she sounded like a stroppy teenager.

"Well, I have a cool story that might help," Mum said eagerly.

Oh, great. Last time you told me a story I ended up having a dream about a space hammer hitting me on the head!

Before Lucy had time to object, Mum began. "There's this thing in the sky called the Hubble Telescope. It's not your average telescope, like people use down here on Earth, it's the size of a school bus! Eleven tonnes to be exact – the weight of two elephants! When I says it's in the sky, I mean it actually orbits the Earth, five-hundred and seventy kilometres above us. It takes just over an hour and a half to circle the whole planet. Pretty amazing, eh kid?"

"Cool," said Lucy.

"I learnt all about Edwin Hubble – the man they named it after – when I was at university. But the coolest thing is that the Hubble Telescope was launched into space in 1990, when I was about your age. It was the reason why I became so fascinated with space."

Lucy could tell how much she loved her job.

"Hubble uses two antennae to communicate with scientists down here on Earth. I wanted to be one of those people! You see, the telescope takes the most incredibly beautiful pictures of things in space we could never imagine. It sees wonderful, magical things. It takes pictures of nebulae – clouds of dust and gas where new stars are born. We also get to see the death of stars, something very powerful and spectacular. The coolest thing Hubble shows us is new and faraway galaxies. This makes us all so excited!"

Her expression grew serious as she caressed Lucy's forehead. "But at the start, it needed some help with seeing. Inside, right in its heart, there are large mirrors that act like eyes. It uses light to see, and in the beginning it struggled through blurriness, just like you. It needed glasses, just like you."

A gentle snore hummed from Lucy's pillow.

"Good night my Lucky Lucy," Mum whispered in her ear as she pulled the duvet up over her shoulders and under her chin.

Sound asleep, Lucy rested. At least tonight there would be no nightmare to wake her from her deep sleep, right?

5

HULA HOOP

BANG BANG BANG!

Lucy jumped awake and flung off her duvet. With a hazy head, she slithered to the side of the bed and sat there for a moment.

Argh, I've still got my school clothes on.

As she reached for her pyjamas, which were sitting on top of the monstrous pile of washing on the floor, she was halted by a strange rattling sound coming from downstairs. She wasn't quite awake enough to remember the night before.

It's that stupid door again, I wish Dad would fix it.

She knew she wouldn't be able to sleep with the annoying rattle, so she dropped her PJs and shuffled down the stairs and into the laundry. The back door was still and quiet. She stopped for a moment, and remembered – *last night had just been a dream, hadn't it?* The moment turned into a while as she gathered her thoughts. And longer, until her heart began to race uncontrollably.

The back door began to rattle again …

She felt its pull. It was telling her to reach for the handle and open it, but she was frozen with fear. Then, something began to tug gently on her sweatshirt, drawing her centimetre by centimetre closer to the back door. It was like being pulled towards a magnet. She tried to resist, but it was impossible.

As she reached the door, it stopped rattling and swooped open, as if inviting her in. She reached out her arms in an attempt to block the invisible force, but it was no good. She braced her feet against the doorframe, but the magnetic energy was too strong. As Lucy entered the black void beyond the door, she closed her eyes tight. With one final tug, the overpowering force swallowed her into nothing.

All was quiet. Lucy reluctantly opened her eyes, unveiling the familiar sight. *I'm back, but where exactly am I?*

She was floating in the darkness like a paper lantern let go in the night sky. The lights were back, millions upon millions of tiny jewels sparkling all around her. Lucy felt like she was swimming deep under water. She breast-stroked through the darkness for a while, then turned around to see the sight of all sights … Earth! Green and brown lands, mountain ranges, and blue oceans wound around the planet – a magnificent view.

This can't be real, I'm dreaming again.

"HELLO!" Lucy mouthed a yell, but there was no sound. She poked at her ears as if there was something stuck in them.

She tried again. "HELLO!"

Nothing but silence.

Below her, unfamiliar objects of varying sizes were whizzing past, again and again.

They're circling the Earth, just like Mum said.

She swam some more, being careful to stay out of the streams of space junk. She felt free, like the ultimate astronomer, exploring things most people could only read about.

Lucy watched a large shiny object speeding away from her.

What's that? Could it be …?

It was like a massive roll of tin foil, with Lego flaps for wings. It looked like her Year 4 science project!

It's the Hubble Telescope, and it's orbiting, which

means it will be back!

Lucy's fear had now turned to curiosity. *If it's just a dream, then I can't get hurt, I need to see it up close!*

While she waited for it to come around again, Lucy came up with a plan. *That's it, the antennae! I can grab hold of one and climb onto its back.*

She remembered her mum telling her it took an hour and a half to circle the Earth, but could already see it in the distance, racing towards her, light reflecting off its metallic skin. Time worked differently in dreams, obviously.

Lucy watched it get closer and closer …

Okay, you got this, it's coming, it's coming. One … two … three …

Got you!

Lucy let out a silent "YEEHA!" as she grabbed the antenna and was whisked away with Hubble into orbit. Hand over hand she moved along the antenna until she reached the cylinder-shaped telescope. Grasping the yellow handrails she guessed were used by astronauts making repairs, she slowly slid herself onto the telescope's back. Then, securing her feet under two smaller rails, she straightened her body. It was like she was surfing on Hubble, along Earth's very own hula hoop!

As Hubble made its way around the planet, Lucy marvelled at every breathtaking view. Daytime, night-time; daytime, night-time – the light changed continuously as the sun played a cheeky game of hide and seek.

Without warning, a sharp burst of light bounced off one of the solar-panelled wings, hitting Lucy smack bang on the face. In her panic to shield her eyes, her feet came out of the rails and she floated off the back of Hubble. She closed her eyes and let out a silent scream, "AAAAH!"

"Lucy! Lucy, what's wrong?" Dad reached down and picked her up off the laundry floor. She opened her eyes, struggled free from his clutches, and whipped open the back door. The backyard was bathed in early morning sun.

"Honey, did you fall asleep in here?" Dad was trying to make sense of her strange behaviour.

"I-I don't know," Lucy stuttered.

"Well you had a hard day yesterday, so you were probably sleepwalking. It's early but I'm off to work, so best you go and get some more rest before school, okay?"

"Okay, Dad." She didn't have the energy to tell him the truth. She dragged herself up to her room and flopped down on her bed, exhausted.

I have to tell Mum.

And with that, she fell into a deep dreamless sleep, until …

BEEP BEEP BEEP!

Argh no! It's Saturday, go away!

6

THE PROOF

"MUM, MUM, MUM!" Lucy screeched down the landing and into her parents' room. She found Mum putting on her favourite royal blue pencil skirt, matched perfectly with a crisp white shirt. *She always looks so nice.*

"Mum, something really weird is happening when I go to sleep … I wake up … and then the door takes me … and I go to space … and there's stars everywhere … and I rode on Hubble, and …" Lucy stopped rambling when she saw the baffled look.

Mum reached out her hand and placed it

on Lucy's forehead. "Are you unwell, sweetie?"

"No, Mum, listen, please. I went to space and I saw–"

"I think your eyes are really causing you some problems, Lucy. You need those prescription glasses sooner rather than later, I think."

Before Lucy could object, Mum hurried out of the bedroom, calling, "Sorry sweetie but I'm late, I've got to go. I'll be home by lunch!"

The front door slammed shut, leaving Lucy standing in her own whirlpool of crazy.

Hubble was there. I touched it, I saw how it was made and how it flew. Maybe if I draw what I saw, Mum will see that I'm telling the truth. It can't have just been a dream …

In her room, Lucy had an old writing desk that slanted at the front – it was great for drawing. It had belonged to her great grandmother, and Mum had used it when she was a kid too. It had little cubby holes which, in the old days, were used for keeping pens and ink.

In the first cubby hole, Lucy kept a stack of scrap paper which Mum brought home from work. In the second were her pencils and a little green frog sharpener, which caught the shavings in its bottom. (Just as well, because Mum hated it when she left them all over the floor.) In the third was a mixture of coloured pencils and crayons, most of which were in pieces but still usable.

Lucy set to work recreating what she'd seen. In the middle of a piece of paper she drew two cylinder shapes, one wider than the other, and joined them together in the middle to look like a telescope. She rummaged through her crayons to find the perfect metallic grey, putting it aside for later. She needed to draw in the bright yellow handrails first. Some were as long as her legs, but the ones she'd slid her feet under had been no longer than a foot-long sandwich.

The antennae were next – one stuck up and one stuck down. She'd got a good look at the one under the belly when she'd climbed up it. The antennae were really long; they looked like two telephone poles strapped to a school bus. On the ends were what looked like dinner plates, moving like spinning tops, only much slower. She coloured those in dark grey.

Next were the Lego wings. Mum was never going to believe her when she said they had Lego wings, so she only had one option …

Lucy knocked on Zac's door. (This was unusual – she usually just barged in.)

"WHAT?" Zac yelled.

"I need to ask you something."

"Well, come in then."

That was surprising. Zac didn't usually let her in his room.

The walls were blue with a green stripe

around the top. The room smelled like rotten fruit and dirty gym clothes. *Open a window you stinky skunk.*

"Can I use that for a sec?" Lucy pointed to the tablet charging on his bedside table.

"Heck no, not a chance, goggles."

Just the reaction Lucy had been expecting. "Well, can you just find something out for me?" she asked in her fake-sweet tone.

"Argh! Quickly then. What?"

"Those wing things on the Hubble Telescope. What are they?"

"Ha, Mum's been telling you her work stories, hasn't she? I got all of those too – so lame."

"Wait, she told you stories too? Did weird things happen? I mean, did you have strange dreams?" Lucy was flustered.

"What are you talking about? Geez you're an oddball, Lucy!"

Just me, then.

"They're solar panels," said Zac. "They power the telescope by converting sunlight into energy. Okay, now get out!" he barked.

Lucy went back to her drawing. She felt silly calling them wings. Of course they weren't wings – but it was kind of cool to imagine the telescope flying through space.

She found a brown colouring pencil, the shade of a rusted pipe, and dug through her school bag for a ruler. She drew two muesli-bar-shaped panels on each side of the telescope's body, and filled each space with small rust-coloured squares.

There, that looks right. Now for the ... eye patch.

She carefully sketched a half oval shape at the end of the smaller cylinder – it was shaped just like a hobbit door. She didn't know what it was for. *That will do nicely.*

Lucy looked at the clock, wondering if she

had time to get crafty with tin foil. *Nah, Mum will be home soon.* She grabbed the metallic grey crayon she'd set aside earlier and filled in all the white spaces.

"There, done," she said proudly. *Oh, no wait.* She took a black crayon and drew a squiggly line off the bottom antennae; she had noticed a loose cord dangling down that was obviously out of place. *Now I can show Mum, and she will definitely believe I've really been there!*

Lucy held the picture under her armpit as she bunny-hopped down the stairs and into the kitchen. She pulled out a breakfast bar stool and sat down, patiently waiting for Mum to arrive home. She hated waiting, especially when she was nervous about something, but it wasn't long before she heard the car pulling into the driveway.

Okay, here we go. I know she'll believe me this time.

7

THE IMPOSSIBLE BELIEF

"Hey, Mum," Lucy said nervously. *I'd better wait for her to make a coffee first.*

Mum hated it when the kids bombarded her with things when she'd barely set foot in the door. Lucy needed her to be in listening mood for sure!

"Oh, hey honey, you feeling better?" she replied lovingly.

I'm not sick, Mum.

"Um, yeah, I'm fine. I want to show you something, but you can make a coffee first." Lucy was doing her best to create the right mood. Mum smiled and flicked on the kettle. Leaning on her elbows over the breakfast bar, she took the picture from Lucy's sweaty hands.

"Ah, I know what this is. How wonderful! You've captured Hubble in such a brilliant way, sweetie."

"Look, I'll show you." Lucy darted around the breakfast bar and leaned into Mum. "Here, see, these are the antennae, and look, here are the solar panels." Lucy proudly showed off her knowledge. Mum nodded and smiled admiringly.

As Lucy's excitement grew, she spoke more and more quickly, describing each part of the telescope in detail as she pointed it out on the drawing.

"This door at the front opens and closes just like the shutter on a camera," she explained, feeling super smart.

"I can't believe Zac let you use his tablet," Mum said. "He must be going soft despite all those workouts." She laughed at her own joke.

Lucy was having none of it. "Oh no, Mum, I drew this all from memory." She couldn't hold it in any longer. "I tried to tell you this morning. I went into space and I saw the Hubble Telescope, I truly did!"

Mum looked at her like she was a puppy in a pet shop window. "Aw, Lucy. You've done some fantastic research – be proud of your hard work."

As the sound of the kettle boiling got louder and louder, Lucy could feel her anger bubbling and creeping up from her tummy.

"THERE'S A PORTAL!" she yelled.

"LUCY!" Mum barked in her most stern parental voice.

Tears started welling up in Lucy's eyes. She tried with all her might to swallow the anxious hiccups she got every time she cried. Her shoulders jumped as she managed to hold one in.

The silence had become unbearably awkward. Mum sighed and gave her "that look" again. *Oh great, she's about to throw me a pity party.*

"You have a great imagination, Lucy, but you have to learn when to stop. Why don't we turn it into a story? Great imaginations make for great stories!"

Lucy stood there silently, her head down.

"Come, sit here," Mum said, tapping the chair next to her. "Let me finish my story about Hubble from the other night, and you can use that to help with your own story." She reached for Lucy's hand.

"NO!" Lucy yelled, pulling away from her grasp. "I'LL SHOW YOU THEN! Come with me!" She stomped down the hall and into the laundry, Mum following with equally heavy feet.

Lucy flung the back door open and jumped through. She landed knees-first on the back step.

"Oh, for goodness sake." Mum picked

Lucy up off the step and brushed the dirt off her knobbly and now grazed knees. She guided her gently into the lounge and onto the couch. "Let me make you a hot chocolate and we can talk about this later."

Lucy lay there, feeling defeated. She thought back to those two wonderful nights; she desperately wanted to believe they were real – real space adventures.

But in that moment, she decided to stop believing. *No more strange sounds or scientifically impossible invisible portals. No more childish pictures, and definitely no more of Mum's stupid space stories!*

8

FOAM PIT FIASCO

Sunday mornings were always lazy in Lucy's household. No-one was ever in a rush to get up, so it was mid-morning by the time they trickled one by one into the kitchen, looking to satisfy their grumbling bellies.

Mum made the coffee while Dad put some bread into the toaster. It was everyone for themselves.

"I have a little thing planned for us this afternoon," Dad piped up.

On a Sunday? Lucy was surprised.

"Oh yeah, we're going to that gymnastics

meet, eh Dad?" Zac joked.

"Ha ha, you're so funny," Lucy responded, but there was a smile on her face. She knew the gym incident would linger for a while, Zac squeezing every last giggle out of the subject.

"We got called to a job at this new development out west yesterday," said Dad, "and I saw this new Jump Skillz place. It's a warehouse full of trampolines – could be fun, eh?"

"Yeah, mean as!" Zac said, with far too much enthusiasm for a Sunday morning.

"We could stay home and let the boys go, Mum?" Lucy suggested.

"Oh no, I want to go!" Mum replied, just as enthusiastically as Zac.

Argh, I'd rather just go back to bed.

"Let's aim to get there at one o'clock, eh team?" Dad said.

Everyone looked at Lucy. "Yeah, whatever."

Bang on one o'clock (because Dad had this uncanny ability to be on time – down to mere seconds), they arrived at Jump Skillz. Inside was a large sign showing two pairs of feet – one bare, with a big red cross over the top, and the other wearing multi-coloured socks. You didn't have to be a genius to work out what the rule was!

Zac took off his trainers, unleashing his putrid-smelling socks.

Dad bought a pair of special Jump Skillz socks. "Look, these have grips on the bottom!" he squeaked, like an overexcited kid.

Lucy slid her ballet flats off and tucked them neatly under the seat she was sitting on with Mum. "They're going in the foam pit," she said, as the boys bolted off. "Should we just go on the normal trampolines, Mum?"

"Hang on, honey, I just need to make a couple of quick phone calls first. I'll meet you over there," she replied.

Argh, not again!

"For goodness' sake, Mum!" Lucy blurted out. She didn't usually get cross in public, especially at her mother, but she'd been over this family day before it had even started!

Mum frowned and was about to respond when the person on the other end of the phone picked up.

Oops, that was lucky.

Ten minutes passed and Mum was still on the phone. Lucy bounced over to where Dad and Zac were flipping into the foam pit, and watched unimpressed from the side.

"Give it a go, Lucky!" Dad pointed to the launch spot.

"Nah, I can't do that!"

He yelled back with his standard motivational line. "Ah nup, kid, there is no such thing as can't!"

Lucy reluctantly climbed up the three

metres or so to stand on the launch spot. She had absolutely no intention of jumping off into the pit. "I'll just watch," she said.

Then, out of nowhere, Zac rushed up behind her and with one big shove, pushed her over the edge and into the foam pit. Unfortunately, as she flung her arm out, she knocked her wrist on the edge of the pit.

"Ow, Zac!" she screamed as she tried to clamber out, clutching her left wrist.

Dad rushed over, grabbed her under the armpits and pulled her up and out. He wrapped his arm around her and led her over to where Mum was still seated.

"Hang on, I'll call you back," she said, taking the phone from her ear. "What on earth happened, Lucy?"

Lucy's face was covered by her hair, and her shoulders jumped uncontrollably as she tried to talk through her tear-filled sobs. "Z-Z-Zac pushed m-me," she stuttered.

"Hard-man" Zac had gone, and in his place was a regular, ashamed fifteen-year-old boy, remorse written all over his face. Mum and Dad looked squarely at him, both shaking their heads. Lucy knew he'd have to pay later – but right now, they needed to get her to a doctor.

"Just hold it up like this, against your chest," said Mum. She then wrapped her leopard-print scarf around Lucy's neck, slipping her injured arm through the middle for support.

It was only a ten-minute drive to Abeltown's accident and emergency department. The car ride was mostly silent, with just a few muffled sniffles escaping as Lucy did her best not be a wimp. As they pulled up to the hospital, Mum suggested crossly that Zac should stay in the car.

"I'll wait here with him. Text me if you want me to come in," said Dad.

Lucy and Mum sat patiently in the waiting room.

Two hours, an uncomfortable examination and an x-ray later, Lucy left the hospital with a fluorescent pink cast (thoughtfully chosen to match her bedroom duvet!).

"A broken wrist, I'm afraid," said Mum as they got back into the car. "It's not too bad, a small fracture, six weeks to heal and it will be just fine."

Zac couldn't bring himself to look at Lucy.

Poor Zac, he didn't mean to hurt me. Maybe I should say something.

But she didn't.

9

GLASSES OF HOPE

"No school for you today," said Mum, filling Lucy's bedroom with light as she pulled back the curtains on Monday morning. She set down a stack of books on the bedside table. "I'd like you to rest that wrist in bed today," she said, gently propping Lucy's arm up on a big fluffy pillow. "I've brought you some books from work, all about space and Hubble – since you seem so interested in it."

Lucy knew Mum hoped she'd become a scientist too. It was highly unlikely that Zac would!

"I don't care about that stuff," Lucy huffed.

Mum looked disappointed. "Well, if you change your mind …" She tapped her hand on the pile of books and turned for the bedroom door.

"Love you," Lucy said, catching her Mum's eye before she left. *I shouldn't be so grumpy with her.*

"I love you too, Lucy."

The doctor had instructed her to stay home for the whole week. "Rest, rest, rest," the adult motto seemed to be. *How boring. Thank goodness Dad's installed a TV in my room. At least I can watch lots of old DVDs to pass the time.*

Nanny McPhee had begun for the second time when Mum came home for lunch. "Hey, how are you feeling?" she asked, sitting carefully on the side of Lucy's bed.

"Bit sore."

"It will be sore for a couple of days, darling. Here, I bought you your favourite lunch," she said, handing her a brown paper bag. The bag was hot and greasy, and from the smell, Lucy knew what was in it without even looking!

"Yum, hot dogs are my favourite! Thanks, Mum." She took a big bite and savoured the taste of fatty batter. Mum didn't usually buy her hot dogs because they were "terribly unhealthy." *She must feel sorry for me.*

"Here." Mum was holding out a purple oval case. Lucy took it with her right hand and awkwardly tried to flip it open.

"Here, let me help," Mum chuckled. She flipped up the top part to reveal Lucy's brand-new glasses. The frames were dark purple and black – Lucy had chosen them herself. *I must have been in quite the sombre mood!*

"Do you like them?" Mum asked anxiously.

"They're okay."

"You'll get used to them, honey." Mum

took them out of the case and slipped them over Lucy's eyes. "Oh, yes. Wow. I think they look amazing. You look beautiful!"

Lucy managed a hint of a smile. "Can I have a mirror?" she asked.

Mum took out her hand mirror from her handbag and handed it to Lucy, waiting for her reaction. Lucy held the mirror up to her face. She turned her head slightly from side to side, getting a good look from every angle. She couldn't stop the smile that was slowly ungluing her pursed lips.

"They are pretty cool," she admitted.

Mum's face relaxed a little.

"Give those books a go, eh?" she said, lifting herself off the bed.

"Maybe."

Mum rummaged through her handbag with her back turned. At the door, she turned around – she was wearing her own new pair of red-framed glasses. "Only cool people wear glasses, Lucy!"

"Oh, Mum. You're such a dork!"

She always makes me feel better.

When the credits of *Nanny McPhee* ran for the second time that day, Lucy reached for the remote and switched off the TV. She sat for a moment before glancing over at the pile of astronomy books still sitting on her bedside table. She read some of the titles:

Expanding Universe, by Owen Edwards.

The Search for Earth's Twin, by Stuart Clark.

Hubble Vision, by Carolyn Collins Petersen. *(Trust Mum to pick that one!)*

Lucy attempted to slide *Hubble Vision* out with one hand. Not surprisingly, the top two books slid off and fell to the floor. She opened *Hubble Vision* and began to read. The words were much clearer than usual. *Huh, maybe this glasses thing isn't so bad after all.*

Lucy spent the afternoon engrossed in the book and its magical pictures – copies of Hubble's famous images.

She got up for dinner, but was soon back in bed reading again. As night fell and her room darkened, she started to experience something she hadn't felt in a few days – excitement. She closed her eyes and flashed back to those millions of sparkling stars. "I need to go back," she whispered to herself.

Lucy sat on the end of her bed, making sure her arm was secure in its sling, and waited anxiously until she was sure everyone had gone to bed. When the house was silent, she gently opened her bedroom door and sneaked, like a ninja in the dark, down to the laundry.

Her heart beat with excitement as she opened the back door wide …

Lucy's shoulders sank and her heart slowed

in disappointment; there was no magnetic force. No space. Just that stray cat lurking in the bushes.

A deflated Lucy headed back upstairs. *Maybe I'll try again tomorrow night.*

The next four nights followed the same pattern. Ninja sneak … back door … nothing.

Night after night after night …

Lucy lost hope of ever travelling through the portal again. *It's gone forever.*

10

THE BIG FIX

It was Saturday night. Lucy and her family were sitting in the lounge eating pizza and watching the rugby. Dad was sporting his team colours, and Mum sipped wine on the couch, taunting Dad with her annoying commentary. Zac was mowing through the pizza.

"Carb loading day is it, Zac?" Lucy said, egging him on.

"You'd better hurry up, pipsqueak, or you'll miss out," he whipped back.

Lucy loved nights like this, everyone being home and just hanging out.

"Go, Go, Go!" Dad yelled at the television.

It can't hear you Dad!

"Woohoo, you beauty!"

Lucy looked at Mum and they laughed at his animated cheers.

"Shall I tell you that story about Hubble's mirrors tonight, Lucy?" Mum asked in a rare moment of calm.

Lucy thought for a moment. *I kind of miss her stories.* "Sure, that would be cool."

"You going to use diagrams and charts, are you, Mum?" Zac joked through a mouthful of pizza.

"Oh, would you like to join us, Zac?" Mum bit back with lightning speed.

She would make a great lawyer.

The room was silent for a moment, and then they all erupted like cackling hyenas!

It was late when Mum finally joined Lucy under her duvet. She had read a lot about Hubble from the books Mum had given her, but she was looking forward to this story.

"Things don't always go the way we want them to in life, Lucy," said Mum. "I know you're not keen on wearing glasses, but lots of people need to. Not just people, actually – even massive space telescopes!"

"Ha ha, that's strange," said Lucy, picturing a telescope wearing an oversized pair of purple and black glasses.

"Yes, odd, isn't it? Let me start from the beginning. I've told you about what Hubble can do, but I haven't told you about its disastrous beginnings. In May 1990, Hubble took its first picture – a star, one thousand three hundred light-years from Earth. The image was mostly black, with white smudges on it. The scientists weren't worried, though; this was just the first test picture to make sure all the equipment was working properly.

"But soon after this, they realised there was something wrong with Hubble – very wrong. They discovered a small fault in the main mirror, and this had massive consequences for the images. They were all blurry! Some very smart people at NASA came to the conclusion that the concave mirror – the mirror that was curved inwards – was too shallow by the tiniest of fractions. It was a devastating discovery. People were really sad, and very angry."

Lucy imagined all the scientists lined up outside Mrs Priers' office, waiting to be scolded!

"Over the next couple of years scientists and engineers came up with an extraordinary plan to fix Hubble. They needed to give it glasses! New instruments were made, which would work just like big spectacles. Then, in 1993, a very brave group of astronauts in the space shuttle *Endeavour* went up to pay Hubble a visit. They did a spectacular space walk and gifted Hubble not one, but five pairs of new mirrored glasses. These glasses were super special – they worked with the faulty mirror to give Hubble the best eyesight ever! Soon, everyone down on Earth was smiling again. Do you know why?"

"Because Hubble sent them cool pictures?" Lucy guessed.

"Absolutely! The pictures were clear and magnificent!" Mum looked at her. "Hubble is amazing, and so are you my darling."

She was right, the story really did help Lucy. "I think I'll wear my glasses now, Mum."

"That's enough talking for tonight," Mum said, rolling over and tickling Lucy under her armpits.

"Argh, ha ha, Mum! Stop, stop!" Lucy shrieked.

Mum jumped out of bed. They said their goodnights with beaming smiles.

"Maybe you could come to work with me

one day and check out the Hubble replica pieces we have on display?" Mum suggested before closing the door.

"That would be cool."

Lucy sunk back into her pillow. *Hmmm, I wonder if I'll dream about Hubble tonight.* And with that thought, Lucy was asleep.

11

THE EAGLE

Lucy woke to find her room still filled with darkness. It was eerily quiet. She listened for the banging noise that she hoped had woken her from her deep sleep.

Nothing.

She got out of bed, put on her blue oversized cardigan, and leaned her ear up against her bedroom door. She stood there for a few moments, holding her breath, longing for a sign that something was happening in the laundry.

Still nothing.

She let out a long sigh of disappointment

and turned back to her bed.

She stopped, suddenly, momentarily blinded by a light whizzing past her window. She rubbed her eyes and stumbled over to look out. There was nothing of interest outside, just a few parked cars and a single street lamp casting light and shadows. Lucy looked at the time shining from her alarm clock, shrugged, and got back into bed.

After more than an hour of staring at the ceiling, she felt her eyelids growing heavy. *Finally.* But her last blink was interrupted by another sharp flash of light bursting through her window. Lucy scrambled up and ran to look out. This time she caught sight of the light fading away, high up into the night sky.

What on Earth was that? Her brain ticked. "It couldn't have been …?"

She grabbed her drawing of Hubble off her desk, found a pen, and looked over at her alarm clock. She wrote down: *1.29 a.m.* That was when she'd seen the first flash of light. *It's now 3.06 a.m. That's, um ...* Lucy did her best to work out how many minutes between each flash of light. She wrote down: *97 minutes.* Excitement started to gently boil up inside of her.

She felt around under her bed, searching for one of the Hubble books that had fallen off her bedside table. Finding it, she flicked to the index at the back, and moving her finger down the list found: *Earth Orbit, Page 54.*

"Hubble orbits our planet in around ninety-seven minutes ..." she read.

OMG!

"If you are looking at the right spot, at the right time, you may even see it with the naked eye. But this can be difficult. Your best bet is to use a telescope and aim it just beyond where you expect to see Hubble."

Lucy was confused. *How can it shine light into my bedroom? Wait, I've got it. It's calling me back!*

Her eleven-year-old imagination shooed away the science that challenged the magic; the impossibility of Hubble shining a light through her window didn't matter. She dropped the book and raced downstairs and into the laundry. Without a hint of doubt, she opened the back door and leapt into the invisible magnetic force that, this time, took her willingly back to space – back to her Hubble.

Lucy found herself flying in orbit again, and she was not alone. Gleaming magnificently in front of her was Hubble, perched on a white space shuttle with the name *Endeavour* written on the side. *The one Mum told me about!*

She tried to push herself closer to the orbiting space shuttle. She could see an astronaut, in a bright white bulky suit and backpack, attached to a long metal arm. The arm looked like it was in a silent dance with Hubble. She tried to yell out, and then remembered the silence of space. Mum had once told her there was no air in space, nothing for sound to travel through. Lucy often wished for this at home, when Zac got on her nerves.

She saw a second astronaut, keeping a tight hold on a tangle of tethers. She had read about how complicated the tethering system was – it needed to be, because it had to stop the astronauts from floating away into oblivion!

Lucy waved to the astronauts, but they didn't see her.

She glided closer and closer to Hubble, until she could see the wide-open double doors on its side. The astronauts were putting things in there – boxes and instruments. *I wonder when they are going to give Hubble its new glasses, like Mum said.*

As she watched, Lucy finally understood how she had come to be in space with Hubble. The stories – Mum's stories. Her words were powering the portal. *I know what the astronauts are doing, because Mum told me in her story last night!*

Now it seemed so obvious: three nights, three stories, three trips to space. *Mum has superpowers!* Lucy wondered if she got them from the lab at the university. So many cool superheroes got their powers via science experiments. *I can't believe my mum is one of them! Maybe she got bitten by a toxic spider, or got stuck in a magnetic space force super experiment machine …*

Lucy's imaginative conclusions were interrupted when she noticed something wasn't quite right with Hubble. *It only has one wing. What have they done with the other one?*

Time appeared to speed up around Lucy, and she saw the astronauts retreat back into the safety of the space shuttle. No sooner were they inside, than Lucy saw two different astronauts emerge from the airlock. Lucy guessed they were only allowed a certain amount of time for their spacewalk, and it was time to swap. They too wore big white suits with square backpacks. Perhaps all this activity meant they were just as concerned as Lucy about Hubble's missing limb!

One of the new astronauts was now attached to the long dancing arm, which moved him high above Hubble, and Lucy saw that he was holding the missing solar "wing" (which, thanks to Mum's books, Lucy now knew was called an array). Then, to Lucy's amazement, he let it go, like an eagle being freed into the wild. It hovered gently in space, high above the Earth.

Lucy gasped in fright as the *Endeavour* pushed away slightly, using its jets, one blast and then a second. The exhaust from the jets hit the array and gently pushed it in Lucy's direction. The majestic eagle brushed over the top of her head, and she closed her eyes. She knew that once she opened them again, she'd be back home. So she didn't. Just for a little longer, she'd stay in the darkness of space, with Hubble and the *Endeavour*.

12

THE RESEARCHER

Lucy skipped happily into the kitchen, "Morning, Mum."

"Hey, Luce," she replied affectionately.

Dad was at work already – what a relief. She couldn't bear the thought of another family "fun day"!

"Do I have to go to school tomorrow, Mum?" she asked through a mouthful of peanut butter toast.

"Looks like you're not in pain, so yes, you do."

Lucy had barely thought about her wrist;

the adrenalin she'd experienced overnight must have made the pain go away.

"I thought you said I could come to your work," she reminded Mum.

"I said one day," Mum replied, sounding a little annoyed.

Lucy couldn't think of an answer to that, so instead she used the puppy-in-a-pet-shop-window look again: *stare and pout, stare and pout.*

Mum gave in. "Okay, fine. Tomorrow after school."

Result!

"Zac can walk you. You can meet me in reception at three thirty."

"Wait, what?" Zac piped up, entering the room.

"You're walking me to Mum's work after school tomorrow," Lucy informed him, as her Mum kissed him on the top of his head on her way out of the kitchen.

"MUM!" he shouted, but she pretended not to hear him. "It's not happening, Lucy. I've got a workout planned, I can't miss leg day."

Lucy laughed, but his expression was serious. It was time for "the look" again: *stare and pout, stare and pout.*

Zac must still have been feeling guilty about the Jump Skillz accident, because he gave in in record time. "Argh, fine. But you can't be late out of class and you'd better get those little legs moving fast."

"Thanks, Zacadoodle." Lucy gave him a quick half hug before he retreated back to his smelly cave.

Lucy sat daydreaming about her overnight adventures. She planned on doing some research about portals and scientific superpowers – the Hubble books wouldn't tell her what she needed to know.

If I'm going to do this properly, then I'm going to need

a device with internet. Who should I ask? Lucy tried to figure out her best bet as she walked up the stairs. Mum's door on the left, or Zac's on the right? There was a good chance that one of them would fall for the *stare and pout* again.

"Knock, knock," Lucy said, tapping her knuckles on the left-hand door.

"Come in."

She pushed the door open a little way and popped her head through the gap. "Hi!" A nervous giggle escaped from her lips.

"Do you need something, Luce?"

Mum had a spare laptop Lucy had been allowed to use just once, when she'd done a science project with her school friend Ardi. Lucy suspected this was only because Mum had been friends with Ardi's dad – a captain in the navy – since high school.

"Oh, um, yeah. Um …" Lucy stuttered, realising she hadn't thought of a good reason for borrowing it.

"Spit it out, Lucy," Mum said impatiently.

"Can I please use the laptop to do some research before the visit tomorrow?" she asked, surprising herself with her own confidence.

"Sure," Mum replied.

Well, that was easy. This conversation has gone much better than I expected!

Mum went into her wardrobe and reached up to the top shelf, pulling down the laptop case. She had a peek inside to check everything was there.

"Here," she said, passing it to Lucy. "You'll need to plug it in, though, it's been up there unused for weeks."

"Okay, yip, I will, thank you."

"You know the rules, eh, Luce?" Mum got anxious when she was online.

"I know," Lucy smiled, doing her best to reassure her.

The laptop didn't sit properly on Lucy's slanting writing desk, so she made space on her bedroom floor to work. The tatty old armchair Mum had had in her first flat, and which now sat in Lucy's room, was in the way of the power point. Lucy heaved the chair forward, just enough to reach around and plug in the laptop cord. She waited a few seconds before pressing the ON button. *Yes, it's working. Oh, wait …* The welcome screen was black with white writing: *UPDATE REQUIRED.* Lucy clicked *OK*, knowing she should do it now, otherwise it would probably interrupt her later.

While she waited, she searched in the mess on her floor for her school bag, finding it dumped next to the week's pile of washing. From the front pocket she took out a small notebook and a pen. (She kept it handy just in case she needed to write a note to someone at school.)

As the update reached fifty per cent, Lucy wrote a few questions in her notebook:

(1) What is a portal?

(2) Can you time travel with magnets?

(3) Human superpowers and labs?

The laptop screen lit up with a magnificent wallpaper of the Milky Way – it was ready. Lucy opened up the web browser and typed in her first question: *WHAT IS A PORTAL?*

Lucy was encouraged by some of the answers she found: "*Doors that you can enter and exit through.*" *That sounds right!* She began to write in her notebook.

When several pages were covered in notes, Lucy moved on to question two, about time travel. She read about a guy named Einstein. His theories about time were complicated, and she couldn't really understand them, but it sounded like he'd travelled in a car with his relative at the speed of light. Lucy laughed. *How absurd!* Then she read something by a guy named Stephen Hawking, about black holes.

They are dark and can suck you into another time and place, she wrote.

That's what the portal is!

Feeling encouraged, Lucy moved on to her last question, and found pages and pages of stories about people getting superpowers from laboratories. She read carefully, noting down specific equipment and chemicals mentioned in the most believable stories. *I must keep an eye out for these in Mum's laboratory.*

Lucy started to squint at the illuminated laptop screen; she looked up and noticed that her room was much darker now. Her grumbling tummy told her it must be dinner time. She closed the laptop screen, unplugged it and placed it carefully back into the case, then slid the notebook and pen back into the front pocket of her backpack. *I'll definitely be needing those tomorrow.*

13

REDDINGTON

Lucy's morning at school was uneventful. Just the usual silent reading and then writing. She was so tempted to write about her Hubble adventures, but decided to keep them to herself – for now.

Lunchtime came around quickly. Bonnie was off sick, so Lucy sat with Ardi under the classroom awnings to eat her honey sandwiches. Ardi was a cute boy (according to all the girls in Lucy's year); his brown hair had natural streaks of blond that got lighter in the sunny months. He was the same size as the other boys his age, but with bigger shoulders. A love of swimming had given him incredible upper body strength.

Lucy was daydreaming about visiting Mum's laboratory that afternoon, when Ardi elbowed her playfully in her side. "Oi you, are you listening?"

"Sorry, I was thinking about something."

"That's okay, Luce"

Lucy immediately felt awful and turned to face him. "Right, I'm listening now. Go," she said with a cheeky smile.

"I was just saying –"

He was abruptly cut off by the sound of the school bell.

"Tell me later, okay? I can't be late to gym class – I'm sure Miss Knuckles hates me," Lucy said as she scooted off.

She made a mental note to catch up with Ardi properly later. *Maybe I could share my secret with him?*

The gymnasium was abuzz with screaming post-lunch kids letting off steam as they waited for Miss Knuckles to arrive. Lucy saw her appear through the gym doors and wince at the loud squeaks of sneakers sliding across the polished wooden floor. It would have been enough to drive any teacher mad.

"Everyone over her and sit down!" Miss Knuckles yelled.

The shrieking and squeaking faded as the children sat down. They were dressed in a mishmash of gym clothes. Frankie, the most popular girl in Lucy's gym class, was wearing the latest Adidas Kids Collection, while Hana, whose family were "alternative", was wearing her dad's tie-dyed T-shirt knotted at the front, and a pair of cut-off denim jeans.

I'd like to see her sprint in those!

Lucy hadn't bothered to get changed. She thought a broken wrist was a good enough excuse not to participate.

"Right, everyone, it's that time again," Miss Knuckles announced. "The Beep Test."

The class groaned.

"Line up on the yellow line, everyone." Miss Knuckles pointed to the back of the hall.

Lucy sat watching the children drag themselves over to the line, racking their brains for any excuse as to why they couldn't do it.

Miss Knuckles wasn't having any of it. "Come on, Lucy," she called out.

"But, Miss Knuckles, I can't. My wrist …" Lucy held up her pink cast, the colour now faded.

"Where's your note?"

Lucy's jaw dropped and she responded nervously, "I didn't think I needed one." *No, Lucy, don't get angry again.*

"I'm having you on, Lucy. Of course you're excused. You can note down your classmates' levels." She handed her a clipboard and a pen.

Phew, she had me going there for a moment. Who knew teachers could be funny!

It was just after three o'clock when Lucy and Ardi walked out the school gate. Before they had a chance to talk, Lucy saw Zac leaning up against the fence post – still looking less than impressed at having to walk Lucy to mum's work.

"We'll talk tomorrow, okay?" Lucy said.

Ardi smiled.

"Hurry up, Lucy!" Zac hollered, spotting her amongst the stampede of kids.

I'm coming, geez. Calm your farm.

Reddington University was in the opposite direction to their house. It was an easy twenty-minute walk from school, through Abeltown's main shops and over a slight rise, into an opening of lush bush and walking tracks. Zac and Lucy cut through the park that surrounded the university. With Zac's "encouragement" they arrived at the steps up to the entrance in just over fifteen minutes.

"There. Go find Mum," he grunted, then he turned and jogged away.

Lucy yelled out a bit of "encouragement" of her own: "Enjoy the cardio!"

Zac didn't stop, but raised his arm in a sarcastic fist pump.

Lucy had only been to Reddington a handful of times, mostly when she was younger. The reception lobby was familiar, but the faces behind the front desk weren't.

"Hi, um, I'm here to see my mum–"

"Hi, sweetie," said a calm voice behind her. "Sorry, I got a bit caught up."

"That's okay, I just got here." Lucy greeted her with a hug. She couldn't hide her excitement as she took Mum's hand and dragged her in the direction of the *STAFF ONLY* door.

It was an old building, and Mum's office

was one of many down a long narrow hallway. They sto- pped for a moment while she got out a swipe card and a set of keys. Continuing through heavy swing doors, they crossed over a paved courtyard and into the science block.

This must be where the laboratories are.

Lucy was showered with countless "Hellos" from passing students, who wore lab coats and smiles.

"Let me show you what we have in here," Mum said, unlocking a nameless door. They entered a dark room. Mum found the light switch, and one by one the old fluorescent tubes flickered on. The large room filled with white light, revealing all of its treasures.

Lucy walked around slowly, gliding her hands over replica parts of the Hubble Telescope. They seemed delightfully familiar. She reached into her bag, feeling around for her picture of Hubble. Finding it, she folded out the creases.

Inspecting each piece, she questioned Mum about where they belonged on Hubble, and exactly what their purpose was. There were a couple of parts she didn't need to ask about – Lucy had read so much about the yellow handrails, their importance and their use. She had already seen the real Hubble, of course! But still, she was happy to see the replica collection down here on Earth.

"Okay, Luce," said Mum. "Let's go into the lab." She handed her a crisp white lab coat, and Lucy didn't hesitate. She put down her bag and slid the coat on over her clothes. It was far too big, and was only a few centimetres off the floor. Mum almost managed to contain her amusement, letting out only a hint of a snort.

"You look like a great astronomer, Lucy!" she said quickly, to recover herself.

Lucy laughed out loud. "I look silly!"

As they entered the lab, Lucy's face fell.

Most of the room was filled with computers and empty desks. *Where's all the big machines and weird looking contraptions?* "Is this it?" she asked, puzzled.

"An astronomers' lab is a place for research and data collection. We've made many great discoveries in here," Mum said proudly.

"Why do I have to wear this silly coat then?" Lucy asked.

"We're scientists, Lucy. We all wear them."

Lucy wandered around the room looking for anything strange; anything that could have turned Mum into a superhuman, but she saw absolutely nothing! A few old telescopes in a corner was about as interesting as it got.

"Where do you look at the stars from then, Mum?"

"Oh, not from here, Lucy. We have a beautiful observatory up on Rose Hill."

Hmmm, that'll be the place.

"Can you take me there?" she asked in her

"sweet" voice.

"Yes, one day," Mum agreed, and before Lucy could get another word in, quickly added, "Not tomorrow!"

Dammit!

Lucy left the science building frustrated that she hadn't uncovered the origin of her mum's powers. But then her thoughts turned to the observatory, and her disappointment melted away – her questions would definitely be answered up there!

"Right, let's go home, eh Luce?" Mum said. They linked arms and Lucy nodded. As they walked through reception, wishing the ladies behind the front desk a good evening, and out into the staff car park, Lucy couldn't help herself. "Mum, can we go to the observatory now?"

"Lucy, no!"

14

CHOCOLATE ISLAND

Lucy lay in bed that night, thinking about the portal's true capabilities. Mum's stories had all been about Hubble and space. Perhaps Lucy would be transported somewhere else, if she got Mum to tell her a story about something completely different. The possibilities were exciting! *Yummy – Lolly Lane, or even better, Chocolate Island!* A scientific experiment beckoned.

It was before "nine o'clock, lights out", so Lucy jumped up and found Mum sitting in bed working on her laptop.

"What are you doing, Mum?" she asked.

"Just work, Luce. I'm really close to proving this new theory."

Lucy could see the exhaustion on her face; dark circles cupped her droopy eyes.

"I can't fall asleep," said Lucy. "Can you tell me a quick story about something silly? Like, um, I don't know – an island made out of chocolate?"

Mum played along, despite her obvious struggle to keep her eyes open. "An island made out of chocolate? How delicious! Okay, then."

Lucy snuggled up.

"A young girl, with eyes that glistened like melted milk chocolate, was lost at sea. She searched and searched for land, until one day she came across a strange-looking island. She docked her boat and stepped into a huge puddle of sloppy mud! It went right up over her gumboots and spilled into her socks. She walked her wet muddy feet further inland, where she discovered a beautiful hut. It would be perfect to stay in. She opened the front door, and found it was filled with every kind of chocolate you could imagine! Dark, milk and white, all muddled together in a delicious pile. Her feet were so sticky that she couldn't walk any further. She took her boots off, and realised that it wasn't mud filling her socks – it was chocolate pudding! Before long, she discovered that the whole island was made of chocolate. She made it her home for just a short while, and when she left she vowed never to tell anyone about her scrumptious chocolate island – because she didn't want to share! The end."

"Ha ha, that was great."

"Off to bed now, Lucy." Mum kissed her on her forehead.

"Good night," Lucy tweeted. She skipped back down the landing and dived back into bed.

I can't wait for the portal to take me to Chocolate Island!

Lucy reached over to her alarm clock and set it for one a.m.

It was twelve forty-five a.m. when Lucy opened her eyes and squinted at the clock. *Perfect.* She hadn't considered earlier that her alarm clock could be heard from her parents' room, and was glad she'd woken up before it went off.

She felt around in the dark and switched it off at the wall. *There, phew.*

Before sneaking downstairs for the portal experiment, she thought about what she should wear. *What would be best for Chocolate Island?* She grabbed a pair of track pants from her bottom drawer, put them on under her nightie and slipped her blue cardigan on over the top. Nice and baggy, with plenty of space left to fill up her tummy with chocolate!

It was cold in the laundry, and Lucy was glad she'd put her cardigan on. She pushed aside

Zac's washing basket, which was blocking the exit to the back door. Her mouth watered in anticipation of melting chocolate covering her tongue.

She opened the back door wide and waited for the magnetic force to take her.

And waited.

And waited a little longer.

Hmmm, what's going on?

She poked her head out into the cool night air. Nothing stopped her; there was no magic in sight. It was a TOTAL MISSION FAIL.

Lucy closed the door and huffed her way into the kitchen – she couldn't go to bed without satisfying her chocolate craving. She remembered Dad had left a Bounty bar in the fridge. "No-one touch it," he'd warned. Lucy wasn't in the mood to care about the consequences, she needed chocolate one way or another!

Stupid portal.

Just as she raised the chocolate to her mouth, she felt a tap on her shoulder. "AH!" Lucy jumped and dropped the chocolate onto the floor.

"Oi, kiddo, that's mine," Dad said.

Lucy playfully slapped him on the arm. "Dad, you scared me!"

"Well you shouldn't be up at this time of night stealing my chocolate!" he scolded. Dad was still in his uniform – home from a late shift.

"Here, want to share?" Lucy tried to give him the piece that had dropped on the floor, but Dad snatched the one still in the wrapper.

"Sure, I'll take this one!"

Argh, smarty pants.

"Go on, Luce, you've got school tomorrow." He gently pushed her in the direction of the stairs.

"Night, Dad," she said, her teeth full of chocolate and coconut.

"Brush your teeth," he said loudly as she

disappeared.

The bathroom was opposite her parents' room at the end of the landing. Light was shining through the gap under the bedroom door. She placed her ear on the door to listen; she could hear the tapping of laptop keys. Lucy decided not to interrupt Mum and went straight into the bathroom.

She liked brushing her teeth, partly because she'd do anything to avoid the dreaded dentist drill, but mostly because she did her best thinking while staring into the mirror.

It must be a hard job being an astronomer. Working all the time, even in bed. I'm not sure I'd want to do that. I'd rather be the chief of a chocolate island tribe! I wonder if Reddington University has a degree in that? Probably something similar.

The portal never took Lucy to Chocolate Island. But not to worry, her dreams did.

15

THE STOLEN HANDRAIL

Another day at school came and went with nothing of particular importance to report. Lucy was in a bad mood after the portal malfunction the night before, so she mumbled her way through the day, slow as a slug. To make it worse, Ardi was absent, and Lucy still felt bad for not making time to talk to him. Not even the smell of frying hot dogs could cheer her up, as she dawdled passed the fish and chip shop on her way home.

Lucy dropped her bag on the floor and collapsed onto the couch, resting her foggy head on a cushion.

The front door slammed, jolting Lucy awake. She sat up, feeling foggy from her unplanned nap. Mum was home, and was rustling around in the fridge looking for something.

"Hi, Mum," Lucy said, sleepy-eyed.

"Have you seen that chocolate that was in here?" Mum snapped.

"Oh, um, yeah. I think Dad ate it last night," she replied.

Well, it's half the truth!

Mum sighed and closed the fridge.

She must be craving chocolate too.

Lucy suddenly remembered the observatory. A visit there would definitely brighten up her day.

"Mum, can we go to your observatory?"

Mum glared at Lucy – but not in a promising kind of way.

Uh oh, she's gonna blow!

Lucy couldn't control the words that came of her mouth next. "You said you would take me." She regretted them immediately. She closed her eyes and gritted her teeth, waiting for the explosion. But it didn't happen. Mum didn't say a word. Instead, she walked slowly over to the couch and sat down, bent over with her head in her hands.

Oh no.

After a moment's hesitation, Lucy shuffled along so she was snuggled next to Mum.

The silence was broken only by little whistles from Mum's nose, as she breathed deeply, trying not to cry. It didn't work for long, though. Mum lost control and her eyes overflowed, tears dripping into the palms of her hands. She slumped against Lucy and sobbed.

Zac walked in then out again just as quickly.

Argh, he's no help.

Lucy rubbed Mum's back, saying nothing. To her surprise, Zac came back in with a box of tissues. "Thanks, Zac," Lucy said, taking them from him.

Zac sat on the single chair opposite the couch and retrieved his phone from his pocket. *I hope he's texting Dad*, Lucy thought. He and Lucy sat in supportive silence.

It was a relief when they heard the front door open. *Phew, Dad's here. He'll know what to do.*

Dad walked into the lounge and glanced at Lucy and Mum, then over at Zac. He seemed to have no idea where to start!

"Hey, honey," he said gently, sitting on the edge of the couch next to her. He took her wet hand in his own and stroked the top of it.

"All my work, all my time, everything wasted," she whispered through her tears.

"What do you mean?"

"It's all wrong – all of it." She began to cry uncontrollably. Dad pulled her into his chest and held her head tight.

Lucy understood. Mum had been working on a new theory for years – one that would change the way people looked at the universe. Lucy knew little about it, but in that very moment, she did know that she couldn't stand seeing her Mum so defeated. She needed to do something. Something extreme, and soon. Luckily, she had a great idea!

Late that evening, when Mum had calmed down, Lucy put the first phase of her plan into gear. "Mum, I was reading about a servicing mission to Hubble, where they ripped off a handrail?" She hoped the questioning tone of her voice would encourage Mum to tell her the story.

"Um, yeah," she replied in a soft, uninterested tone. "A screw got stuck, and after a lot of fast-thinking ground experiments, they decided to basically just rip the rail off."

"Hmm, okay, thanks. I might have to read some more then," Lucy replied.

I hope that'll do it.

Lucy was unsure if Mum's power was strong enough tonight to open the portal once more, but her plan depended on it!

Everyone went to bed early that night, which wasn't surprising after such an emotional afternoon. Lucy waited – still dressed under her covers – for the house to fall asleep. When the snoring symphony began, it signalled time.

Tiptoeing along the landing and down the stairs, Lucy entered the laundry and gently closed the door behind her. She held her breath, nervous that her plan could fail, and opened the back door. She was relieved when the gentle tug of the portal's energy slowly pulled her forward. Closing her eyes, she let it pull her into space, and back to

Hubble. *Phase two complete.*

Phase three was a little trickier. Lucy had hoped to come up with a plan on the spot. Hubble looked the same as on her last visit; it was still perched on a grand white space shuttle. But she noticed that this wasn't the *Endeavour* – the name painted on the side read *Atlantis*.

Lucy looked around in the darkness surrounding Hubble, searching for the astronauts she was hoping to see. She wished she'd put her glasses on, because what she needed to do next was something she wasn't particularly good at – catching!

Lucy swam in closer to watch what she knew was a significant moment in Hubble's servicing history. She had learnt from her books that the astronauts would have trouble removing one bright yellow handrail, and that this was necessary to continue their mission. She waited patiently for what seemed like forever, as they tried tool after tool to release the stubborn screw that had halted their progress. She watched as one astronaut set himself up for the "brute force technique" she had read about, and which Mum had confirmed. He ditched his tools, grabbed the handrail with one hand, leant back and yanked it hard. *SNAP!* It broke off, just like in the history books! The release unbalanced the astronaut for a moment, and he lost his grip on the handrail – which floated out into space.

Phase Three: Get that handrail!

Lucy flapped her arms frantically in the direction of the rail. Every time she got close it drifted further away from her grasp. *Come here! Almost, almost …*

She refused to give up. Her plan depended on getting that handrail!

With her energy fading, she heaved herself forward one last time. Her fingertips grazed a tail-like piece of tape, dangling from the handrail's rear. She reached her other hand forward and managed to get a good grip with both hands. Relieved, Lucy tucked the handrail under her clothes, securing it in the elastic of her track pants.

She looked around and could no longer see Hubble, or *Atlantis*. She could barely even see Earth, now. It was just a tiny blue dot surrounded by darkness and stars.

Oh no! How do I get back?

16

PROOF REPEATED

Alone in space. Far away from the comfort of Earth, and floating into oblivion, Lucy felt her heart beating harder and faster.

What have I done?

Before panic took over her body, Lucy spotted something swirling not far in front of her. It reminded her of when light shone through her bedroom window, revealing millions of tiny dust particles dancing in the air. She shook awake her tired arms, and urged herself through the darkness into the cloud of shining dust.

She drifted with its calm motion; it was like being taken by a current at sea. She felt it moving faster and faster, until she couldn't control the movement of her body, which tumbled and turned in the stream. The gentle spins grew more violent, until she felt like an odd sock spinning alone in a clothes dryer.

Battling to get off the ride, Lucy spotted a sphere of green and blue getting closer and closer. Earth! She lost sight of it briefly as her body was thrown around and around. She caught sight of it again; it was much closer. Lucy started to feel dizzy as the dust stream began to orbit Earth at lightning speed. The magnificent gem colours of emerald and sapphire flashing before her eyes were almost too much to bear. Suddenly a black hole opened up under her feet, and she was quickly sucked in.

"AH!" she screamed as her tummy dropped to her toes.

Her feet landed on solid ground, and her body crumpled to the floor.

Exhausted, Lucy opened her eyes. She had never been happier to find herself lying on the cold laundry floor. Taking a few deep breaths to calm herself, she stood up.

The handrail?!

It was still tucked securely into her waistband. *Phew.*

"Phase Three complete," she whispered to herself. *I don't think I'll be doing that again.*

It was too late for Lucy to continue her mission. She would complete the final phase the next day, by giving Mum the handrail – the proof of her space travel!

The sun darted through the bedroom curtains and over Lucy's face, waking her from a deep sleep. She glanced at her alarm clock. *Oh no!* She'd forgotten to turn it back on two nights back, and now she had no idea what the time was.

She scrambled out of bed to find her watch

in the top drawer of her dresser. *Eight-thirty a.m.* She didn't have time to wonder why no-one had woken her up for school, all she knew was she was going to be late for sure! She quickly changed her clothes, grabbed her bag and tore down to the kitchen.

Zac was there, packing his lunch – a carefully weighed piece of chicken and cold broccoli – into his school bag. "Sorry, none for you, Lucky Ducky, you'll have to stay puny," he teased.

Lucy poked her tongue out at him and grabbed a packet of chips from the cupboard. *This will do.* She stuffed them into her schoolbag.

"Mum's still in bed. I think we should just let her sleep, Luce," Zac said, his face serious for once.

"Yeah," Lucy squeaked in agreement.

"Right, come on then, I'll walk with you."

Zac could be very sweet sometimes. Lucy

was lucky to have him as a big brother – even if he had the worst protein farts!

Bonnie and Ardi were both at school, but neither was talkative. At lunchtime, the three of them sat silently together under the shade of a large oak tree. It was clear they all had things on their minds.

Lucy's wish for the school day to go fast was granted, and before she knew it, she was home again. Mum greeted her with a smile from the kitchen. Lucy was surprised to see her looking so cheery; she'd half expected her to still be in bed.

"Have you had a good day, sweetie?" she asked.

"It was all right, same old stuff," Lucy replied.

She'd spent all day thinking about Hubble's handrail, hidden under her bed. She was anxious to show Mum, but also nervous. It wasn't normal to tell your mum she has superpowers!

It made sense to Lucy that Mum had been chosen as a special person. Here she was, defeated one day and starting over the next. *She's amazing.*

Lucy decided to wait until later to show her the proof of her superpowers.

After dinner, Lucy helped Mum with the dishes. "I'm sorry about your work, Mum."

"It's okay. That's what being a scientist is all about, really. We can't always get it right."

"Can you tell me about it?" Lucy had always been interested in Mum's work – but it had become magical to her now.

"Hmm, maybe I can show you when it gets dark," Mum suggested, looking out the kitchen window into a clear night sky.

Lucy grinned at the offer.

By seven thirty, darkness dominated the sky. Lucy, wearing her snuggly fleece dressing gown, walked with Mum out the back door. They clambered up the trampoline ladder and lay side by side, looking up at the night's beauty. They'd looked at the stars from here since Lucy was a little girl. Then, Mum used to say the stars were fairy bells, and that when they twinkled, they were saying hello. Sometimes the two of them would stay out there for hours, greeting all the friendly fairies.

"See over there, that group of stars with six in a row …" Mum raised her arm and pointed into the sky.

"Yip, I see."

"Well, I've been studying beyond that area of space, and I had concluded that a planet, far, far away, was orbiting not one, not two, but multiple stars," she explained. "We know this to be true for other planets, but we hadn't yet discovered the truth about this one. I was so sure …" Lucy could hear the disappointment in Mum's voice.

"I've got something to show you. It's in my room," Lucy said nervously.

"Okay," Mum said, curious.

Together, they jumped off the trampoline and made their way inside to Lucy's room.

Mum watched as Lucy stretched out flat on the floor and slid herself halfway under the bed. "What are you hiding under there, kid?"

Lucy wiggled her bottom back until her head emerged from under the bed. She pulled the yellow handrail out and sat back onto her heels.

Mum's face changed from wonder to confusion as Lucy handed it to her. She pressed her lips together as she rotated the handrail between her hands, looking at it from every angle. The confused look turned quickly to anger.

"You took this?" she asked.

Before any words could find their way out of Lucy's mouth, Mum barked, "You STOLE this from my work? Really, Lucy, how could you?"

"No, Mum. No!" Lucy geared up to explain, but the opportunity was lost as Mum stormed out of her room, still clutching the handrail.

Lucy didn't have the courage to follow her. She stood still, feeling the full force of gravity holding her in place.

How can this all be going so wrong?

17

THREE SUNS

Mum sat alone under the dimmed kitchen light, staring at the handrail in disbelief. She'd never have thought her daughter could do something so dishonest. It wasn't often she had no idea how to handle a problem, but this was one of those times.

Her brain ticked over, until she spotted something strange. Her eyes squinted at the handrail perched on the breakfast bar. Moving closer, she noticed a small engraved marking on the top of the rail. She held it directly under the ceiling light and saw indented letters, with specs of black still visible: NASA T6 25. She brought it up under her nose and inspected it closer. It was worn and weathered in places. She embraced it close to her chest and allowed her mind to consider the impossible.

"LUCY!" She yelled.

Lucy heard Mum's call, but gravity still held her firmly in place.

"LUCY!" Mum yelled louder this time, sounding more desperate.

Lucy wrestled the anxiety that weighed her down, and broke free. From the top of the stairs she could see Mum standing in the kitchen, holding the rail close, staring up at her. Lucy took each step deliberately slowly, and for a moment, considered bolting out the front door.

"Come here, Lucy, it's okay," Mum said. She was gripping the handrail tightly into her chest, and her eyes were pleading. "I need to know the truth. I know you didn't take this from Reddington, but where did you get it from?" Lucy saw her bracing herself for the answer.

Lucy sucked in a deep breath. "I took it from the real Hubble, in space."

Mum looked down at the rail, shook her head gently in disbelief, and they stood in a moment of silence. She looked back up at Lucy. Her eyes had a different look about them now – they were young, and curious.

Lucy nodded her head slowly up and down, and reached for Mum's hand. "Come with me," she said, leading her gently towards the laundry.

Standing side by side, her bare feet on the cool laundry floor, Lucy looked up at Mum. "Trust me," she said with a confident smile.

Mum's eyebrows lowered, coming closer to her wobbly smile. It was a look Lucy had never seen before. *She's nervous.*

Lucy reached forward and opened the back door wide. The peaceful night air brushed over their faces. Lucy took a step forward, pulling Mum to join her. "Close your eyes, Mum, it's less scary."

Mum took the crisp night air deep into her lungs, and let her eyes close softly. Lucy tugged her from ahead, her body floating as she was pulled through the door. Mum was desperately trying to keep hold of her hand without giving into the energy force that was lapping at her feet.

"No, Mum, let yourself go," Lucy instructed.

Mum took one small step forward and her body slowly started to lift off the floor as she allowed the force to envelope her. Hand in hand they let go of the safety of home and travelled through the portal together, their eyes wide open.

They glided through a storm of glitter and out into a dark, empty ocean. Out of nowhere, Mum let out a contagious laugh. Lucy caught it and they shared the joyful moment. "Wait, I can hear you!" Lucy said in amazement.

"This is incredible!" Mum replied.

Lucy got hold of her dressing gown tie and looped it through the ring in Mum's jeans, and secured them together. "Let's not get separated."

Lucy felt much safer with Mum. The space in front of them was almost completely empty; there were only a few distant shining objects that looked like spinning tops. They turned around to see the full panoramic view, and Mum gasped at the sight. "That's the Milky Way!"

Lucy looked at Mum in wonder. "Is that our galaxy?"

"Yes, that's our home, Lucy," she replied, still in shock.

Lucy stopped to think for a moment. Then she remembered Mum's last story, back home on the trampoline. "I know why we're here," she said. "Your theory, we're here to prove it!" She waved in the direction of the nearest cluster of stars, spinning in the depths of darkness. Lucy spotted another turbulent tube of travelling dust, and could only hope it was their ticket to Mum's three-sunned planet. She grabbed her dressing gown tie and yanked them forward a few metres to slip into the stream.

"Hold on tight, it's a rough ride!" she shouted.

They tumbled and tangled together in the current, until it spat them out in front of a magnificent sight. Catching her breath, Mum whispered in awe, "An extragalactic planet!"

Lucy scrunched up her nose. *This is far beyond my brain power* …

Mum could see that Lucy had no idea what she had just said. "A planet outside of our galaxy, the Milky Way," she explained.

A small droplet of water hit Lucy on her cheek. She swatted it off, in the same way as when Zac flicked a disgusting ball of booger at her. She looked at Mum. Droplets of water were escaping her eyes and bobbling in front of them, like tiny fairy water balloons.

Lucy put her arm around Mum and held her close. "See, you were right." She pointed to three orange masses burning in empty space beyond the planet.

"Three suns ..."

18

VICTORIA

Mum had predicted that the extragalactic planet would be small – about one hundredth the size of Earth – and she was right. The surface was covered in craters; it looked like the Moon. Lucy remembered that the Moon had no atmosphere to shield it from violent collisions with asteroids and the like.

"Can we walk on it?" asked Lucy.

"I think it has a small amount of gravitational pull," said Mum, "so you'd bounce around like you do at Jump Skillz."

Well that's not a pleasant memory …

"Let's go then," Lucy said with a cheeky

131

grin.

"Oh, that's not a good idea, Luce. It would be too hot. With three suns, the radiation would be off the charts."

Lucy tilted her head to the side. "Um, Mum, we are breathing and floating around in deep space in jeans and a dressing gown. And I think we're doing okay!" The absurdity made them both chuckle.

They interlocked hands and made their way closer to the planet. It grew bigger and bigger with every push forward. Feeling as if they were attached to a parachute, they experienced the subtle pull of gravity guiding them to the solid ground. Their toes met the rocky surface of a mountain rise. The small amount of gravity was enough for them to steady their footing, then they wedged their bottoms into in a gap in the rocks to stop themselves floating off again.

They sat admiring the three suns in their

interesting formation.

The largest sun was the "rock star" – the planet orbited around it, accepting its gift of light. The other two stars were much smaller and some distance away from the rock star, worshipping it, and fighting for its attention.

They watched as the large star descended towards the horizon. The minions followed, taking with them the last of the light. Then, Lucy and her Mum were sitting in darkness.

Lucy broke the silence. "You made this happen, Mum."

"What do you mean?"

"Every time you tell a story about space, the portal opens." Lucy was desperate for Mum to understand her own powers.

Smiling, Mum took Lucy's face between her hands. "You are extraordinary, my girl."

Light suddenly beamed from behind them, and they turned to see the first of the three magnificent suns rise above the planet.

Their eyes adjusted to the light as it grew brighter. The smaller suns emerged in its path, and all three appeared to soar up and over the planet, surrounded by the countless other stars that shone distantly from all parts of its galaxy.

"Bit different to the sunrises we see on Earth, eh?" Mum said with a sparkle in her eye.

Time passed quickly. "I think the only way back is to find another tunnely thing, Mum," Lucy said, pointing in the direction they had come from.

Mum laughed. "Tunnely thing? I think we need to come up with some proper scientific names! But first, let's give this magical planet a name, shall we? Lucy has a nice ring to it."

"No, Mum. Victoria. It's your discovery, it should be named after you."

"Okay, Victoria sounds wonderful. I'm so proud of you, kid."

Lucy poked her tongue out at her, unwedged her bottom from the rocks, and pushed off the surface.

"Come on then, old lady," she teased.

Mum fought the grip of Victoria's low gravity, and caught the drift from Lucy's path. Together they searched for a tunnel of dust that would hopefully return them to Earth. "Space tubes, that's what we could call them," Mum suggested.

Argh, adults are so boring …

"Nah, they are galactic time worms!"

"Ha-ha, okay, that sounds great!" Mum giggled. She loved Lucy's imagination.

Lucy spotted one. "Aha, over there, a worm!"

"I hope it's heading back to Earth," Mum said. She looked a little worried that they'd be lost in deep space forever.

"We'll soon find out," said Lucy.

Holding on tight to each other, they slipped into the side of the galactic worm and tumbled once again through its turbulent stream. Lucy's stomach dropped as she fell suddenly through an opening under her feet. She zigzagged through the emptiness like a deflating balloon, her arms and legs waving wildly as she searched for something to halt her descent.

Lucy crashed onto a metallic surface. She had no time to move out of the way before Mum dropped from the darkness straight onto Lucy's back, squeezing the last ounce of energy from her body.

Lucy moved her hands over the smooth shiny surface.

This is not the laundry floor …

Gently untangling herself from Mum's body, Lucy attempted to stand up, like a surfer trying to catch their first wave. She stumbled, so instead stayed kneeling, holding on tightly to …

her dear friend, Hubble! She was back, and so glad to be. She sat watching the Earth pass by, as Hubble continued its orbit.

"Where are we, Lucy?" Mum had finally caught her breath and was looking around her in confusion.

"Sit up slowly, Mum. Here, hold onto this." Lucy guided Mum's hand onto a yellow handrail. She blinked purposefully a few times, adjusting to her surroundings. She seemed mesmerised by Earth's magnificent beauty, as Hubble passed by the vast blue waters of the Pacific Ocean. Mum knew exactly where they were.

Neither had the energy for more words.

Lucy's Mum had always been fascinated with the Hubble Telescope. Now she was kneeling upon it, sharing her love of astronomy with her daughter, and exploring all the wonders the universe had to offer. They rode on the majestic beast through sunrise and sunset, until their eyelids were too heavy to keep open.

Hubble gently released their sleeping bodies into its trail of glistening dust, sending them home to Earth.

19

LOOPY LUCY

"Taking the day off, are we?" Lucy woke to Dad pulling at her toes. She felt as tired as Dad looked after a long nightshift at the fire station.

She sat up and held her pounding head. Next to her lay Mum, snoring peacefully under the covers.

"You two had a sleepover, have you?"

"Ah yeah, girls' night, Dad."

Lucy was still dazed from the night's adventure. The covers started to shift as Mum stretched her body awake. Lucy looked over at the alarm clock, and was confused to see it was already past nine a.m.

"I feel like I've been sleeping for years," Mum moaned, sitting up. "When did you come in, Lucy?"

"Girls' night, Mum. Remember?" Lucy said, flashing a smile up to Dad.

"I'll make you lazy girls some breakfast, shall I?" he said, leaving the bedroom.

Lucy smiled at Mum, eager to talk about their adventures.

"Gosh, we must both have been pooped, Lucy. I crashed out. I don't even remember coming to bed!"

Lucy flopped back down onto the pillow. "Did you have any dreams last night, Mum? Like … about your theory?"

"Strangely, I didn't actually. This was the first night in many that my theory didn't dominate my dreams. I've let it go, I suppose."

Lucy was shocked. *She remembers nothing?*

"What should we do about Hubble's hand-rail?"

Lucy was sure this would bring her memory back.

"What are you talking about? Sounds like you had some interesting dreams!"

"Wait here …" Lucy jumped out of bed and ran downstairs to the kitchen, where Mum had left the handrail. On the breakfast bar sat orange juice and cereal – but no rail.

"Not quite ready yet, Luce," Dad said.

She ignored him, looking on the table, in the lounge, and even under her bed. Nothing. It was gone. Puzzled, she went back to her parents' room and sat down on the side of the bed.

"I know you haven't quite figured it out yet, but your theory is right, Mum. There is a planet with three suns. It's not in our galaxy, though. It's in a smaller one that's orbiting our own Milky Way."

Lucy could see Mum trying to make sense of her words. *She'll probably never believe me.*

"Not in our galaxy, you say?"

"No, it kind of looks like it is, but it's not. The suns are strange too — really it's just one big star, with two annoying ones hanging around like a bad smell."

Mum's face lit up. She grabbed her laptop — she kept it next to her bed for the good ideas that popped into her brain late at night — and frantically typed something.

"I don't know where you came up with that, Luce, but you're onto something! I'll let you know what I come up with, eh? Maybe my theory isn't quite dead."

Lucy leant back, resting on Mum's legs. Looking up at the ceiling, she understood now; it didn't matter if Mum couldn't remember. She was still LUCY THE SPACE ADVENTURER — with the help of Mum's stories, of course!

"You're going to be the woman that discovers everything, Mum," she announced with great confidence.

"Ha, gosh you are loopy, my Lucy!"

A ding sounded from the laptop. Mum clicked into her email inbox. She read silently, her face showing an assortment of expressions.

"What's that all about?" (Lucy could be as nosey as Zac sometimes.)

"A project for the ISS."

"For what?" Lucy didn't always understand science lingo.

"The International Space Station," said Mum.

Oh, I've read about that …

Lucy thought for a moment, then she had a wonderful idea. "Can you tell me a story about the Space Station tonight, Mum?"

"Oh Lucy, not tonight. It looks like I'll be working late since I'm not even out of bed yet!"

Lucy wasn't too disappointed. She needed an early night – she felt like she'd run a marathon to the moon and back!

"Tomorrow night, then?"

"Okay, Lucy."

Yes! International Space Station here I come!

ABOUT THE AUTHOR

 Claire lives in the North Island of New Zealand with her husband, three children, and a dog and cat who closely supervise Claire while she writes.

She has worked in the disability sector and in primary schools, where she gives learning support to children with special education needs. She has always had a passion for writing, and recently won five excellence awards while studying for a Graduate Diploma in Media Studies.

Claire aims through her writing to stir children's imaginations, inspiring them to set their own creative minds free. *Loopy Lucy: Flying with Hubble*, is her debut novel, and the first in a planned series.

ACKNOWLEDGEMENTS

Many people have supported me through my writing journey. Anton, the love of my life, I thank you for your continuous encouragement to follow my passion, even when it felt impossible. A big thank you to Sue Copsey, my wonderful editor, for all the work you put into this book. You made the process incredibly smooth, even when I had a million questions for you! To the super talented artist Sophie, thank you for creating the cover of my dreams. I want to acknowledge and thank my Whanau and community. You have empowered me with your endless support and kindness. Finally, to my children, you woke up my imagination and I will forever share my stories with you.

THE LOOPY LUCY SERIES
BOOK TWO

School's out, and Lucy is excited to return to the cosmic laundry room she's discovered in her house, ready for her next space adventure. The portal opens when her mother tells Lucy stories about her work as a space scientist. Now she wants Mum to tell her about the International Space Station, in the hope that the portal will take her there. But then Dad arrives in a run-down motorhome called Madeline, and announces that the family are going on a road trip. Not only are Lucy's space adventure plans foiled, she's also expected to share a cramped old van with her smelly brother Zac!

Will she survive and find some magic during this trip, or will sharing with Zac lead to disaster?

OUT NOW!

Made in the
USA
Middletown, DE